I'm 5

by Alva Sachs

illustrated by
Patricia Krebs

Three Wishes Publishing Company

Signature Book Printing - www.sbpbooks.com - Printed in the United States.

Illustrations and graphic design by Patricia Krebs

Editor: Cheri Dellelo - www.dellelo.com

First edition published in 2011 by Three Wishes Publishing Company
Three Wishes Publishing Company
26500 West Agoura Road, Suite 102-754
Calabasas, CA 91302
Phone: 818-878-0902
Fax: 818-878-1805
www.threewishespublishing.com

Library of Congress Cataloging-in-Publication Data:
Sachs, Alva.
    I'm 5 / by Alva Sachs; illustrated by Patricia Krebs. -- 1st ed.
    p. cm.
    SUMMARY: Birthday parties, friends, games, and getting ready for kindergarten.
    Sounds like lots of fun! Julie is five and is ready for kindergarten, but kindergarten
    is not yet ready for her. Finally, Julie gets the chance to board the yellow bus
    and go to school with all her friends.
    Audience: Ages 3-8.
    LCCN 2010934742
    ISBN-13: 9780979638022
    ISBN-10: 097963802X
    1. Kindergarten--Juvenile fiction. [1. Kindergarten--Fiction.] I. Krebs, Patricia, ill. II. Title.
    III. Title: I am 5. IV. Title: I am five.

    PZ7.S11852Im 2011 [E]
    QBI11-600027
    To the Agreement dated January 24, 2011, between ALFRED PUBLISHING MUSIC CO. INC.
    and Alva Sachs:
               HAPPY BIRTHDAY TO YOU
    Words and Music by MILDRED J. HILL and PATTY S. HILL
    © 1935 (Renewed) SUMMY-BIRCHARD MUSIC, a Division of SUMMY-BIRCHARD, INC.
    All Rights Administered by WB MUSIC CORP.
    All Rights Reserved - Used by Permission

This story is dedicated to my original three wishes: Justin, Jessica, and Julie, who fill my life with love, joy, and laughter.

"Happy Birthday to YOU!
    Happy Birthday to YOU!
        Happy Birthday, dear JULIE!
            Happy Birthday to YOU!"

Julie counted each candle out loud, "1, 2, 3, 4, 5, 6. Six?"

"Oh, and *one for good luck,*" she smiled remembering
what her mother always said.

Leaning closer to the delicious-looking cake,
Julie took one last glance at the pink, yellow, blue,
and purple flowers. "Yummy!" she thought.

Closing her green eyes as tight as she could,
she took in the biggest breath of air ever
and blew out ALL the candles.

"I'm 5!" shouted Julie, opening her eyes. "Hurray!"

Everyone was clapping and singing. Julie's dad, mom, her brother Joey, her sister Jenna, and her friends, Patricia, Tony, Kim, Luis, and Rashad joined in.

After cake and ice cream, the music started!
Julie and her friends dashed off to check it out.

"Yes, musical chairs!" they all sang out,
jumping up and down.

They chased each other round and round in circles,
each hoping to land on an empty chair
when the music stopped.

One by one, the chairs disappeared as they cheered
each other on.

The birthday celebration continued as Julie and her
friends played Bingo, Pin the Tail on the Donkey, and
then unwrapped presents!

Julie's friends made their way to the front door, with prizes, toys, and candy spilling over the tops of their goodie bags!

"I'm ready for school tomorrow," Julie said looking up with her new, purple backpack hung over her shoulders.

"Well, Julie," replied her mom, "school doesn't start just yet."

"But you said when I am 5, I can go to kindergarten. Well, I'm 5 TODAY," announced Julie.

It was still summer, and Julie had a whole month to wait for school to start.

Julie had no idea how LONG a month was.

All she knew was that she was 5 and she was ready for school. Why wasn't school ready for her?

Julie's dad gave her a hug. "Honey, school will be ready for you in no time, you'll see."

Every day seemed to be the same.

Julie woke up, brushed her teeth, got dressed,
and ran quickly down the stairs to the kitchen.

"Where do you think you're going?"
asked Jenna.

"I'm going to school today."

No, Julie, not today.

"NO, Julie, not today,"
was always the same reply.

Julie turned away and climbed up
each stair one by one retreating to
her bedroom.

This morning, like every other morning, Julie made her way downstairs to the kitchen.

Jenna was waiting for her at the kitchen table.

"Hey, what's that?" Julie asked.

"It's a calendar and I have some crayons too," her sister showed her.

"What's it for?" Julie wondered.

"These are all the days of the week--Sunday, Monday, Tuesday, Wednesday, Thursday, Friday, and Saturday. Let's cross off each of the days until school starts. We can put an X in this box, which is today. When ALL the boxes have an X in them, it will be your FIRST day of kindergarten!"

Giving Jenna a big hug, Julie whispered in her ear, "Cool! You're the best!"

Julie played with her friends.

Julie rode her bicycle.

Julie played with her dog.

Julie played video games.

Julie and the girls played dress-up.

Julie even cleaned her room!

At the end of each day, before bed,
Julie would dance down to the kitchen
in her pajamas, pick out a crayon,
and draw an X in the box for that day.

In no time, the calendar was filling up
with pretty colored X's everywhere!

"What's all this, Julie?" Mom asked one day, peering in the doorway of Julie's bedroom.

"I'm getting my clothes ready for school tomorrow," said Julie. "My calendar is full of X's, and you know what that means? I go to school tomorrow!"

Her dad chimed in too, "Well, is my little girl ready for the BIG DAY?"

Julie answered, "I was ready a LONG time ago, but school was not ready for me!"

That night Julie hopped into bed with her favorite stuffed animal, Max the dog.

"Hey, you want me to read you a story tonight?"
Joey asked peeking in her room.

"Sure," smiled Julie. "But it has to be a short one,
because I have to fall asleep really fast tonight
so I can get up, get dressed, eat breakfast,
and be ready for the bus to take me to
kindergarten in the morning."

Before the story was over,
Julie was fast asleep.

Morning did come quickly!

Julie jumped out of bed and ran to the bathroom
to wash her face and brush her teeth and hair.

She tossed on her clothes as fast as she could and raced down the stairs to the kitchen.

"Here I am!" shouted Julie. "Hurry, we need to get to the corner before the bus gets there! I don't want to be late for my first day of school!"

The sun was shining.

The air was crisp.

You could hear the fall breeze rustling through the trees.

The corner bus stop was crowded with boys and girls ready to start their school day too. A flash of yellow streaked around the corner. Julie's heart began to beat faster and faster.

The BIG YELLOW BUS appeared!

The bus stopped. The doors swung open.
Everyone stepped up to get on board.

It was a very BIG step for Julie,
but she made it.

Julie looked out the window.
"This is going to be the best day ever!
School IS ready for me!"

Alva Sachs earned her Bachelor of Science degree at the University of Illinois and her Master of Education degree from Northern Illinois University, and has more than sixteen years of teaching experience. Her life-long passion has been writing for kids. Her days in the classroom provided the inspiration for becoming a children's writer. In 2007, she published *Circus Fever*, which has been selected as a finalist for the 2009 Indie Excellence Award and the 2009 Best Books Award, received a 2008 Hollywood Book Festival Honorable Mention, the 2009 Seal of Excellence from Creative Child Magazine, and the 2010 Eric Hoeffer Award for Excellence in small press publishing. Right after the success of her first book, she published *On Your Mark, Get Set, Go!* It has been awarded with the 2010 Seal of Excellence from Creative Child Magazine and was selected as a finalist for the 2010 Indie Excellence Award, and the 2010 International Book Award. Reading her stories in person at a variety of venues and public events, has opened up a whole new "classroom" for Alva. Her complete dedication to the mission of sharing the fun of reading has brought her a wonderful gift in return: experiencing how the young audience and their families enjoy, participate, and become interested in the whole process of creating a story. Being a board member of Reading Is FUNdamental of Southern California has also allowed Alva to foster literacy by helping families to build home libraries. Visit Alva at www.alvasachs.com.

Patricia Krebs is a multimedia artist who grew up in Buenos Aires, Argentina, where she earned a degree in Fine Arts Education at Rogelio Yrurtia National School of Fine Arts, a degree in Painting at Prilidiano Pueyrredón National School of Fine Arts, and a degree in Contemporary Visual Arts at IUNA (National University of Arts Institute). Since her first publication in 2006, Krebs has illustrated and designed several award winning children's picture books, including *Zee... Adventure One: Borrowing China; Circus Fever; Classic Songs, Rhymes and Activities in English, Spanish and ASL;* and *On Your Mark, Get Set, Go!* Her works received recognition from organizations such as the International Board on Books for Young Children (IBBY) and the Department of Cultural Affairs of the City of Los Angeles, among others. Her paintings and sculptures are exhibited internationally in galleries, commissioned by collectors, and featured in books, on CD covers, and in educational publications like *Decisio* (sponsored by UNESCO). In addition, she creates puppets, masks and props for theatrical events, writes lyrics and music for her own musical projects as well as for other artists and companies, and records Spanish voiceovers for major movies, such as *Happy Feet, Harry Potter and the Goblet of Fire, Corpse Bride,* and *Beowulf.* Visit Patricia at www.patriciakrebs.com.ar.

Alva (L) and Patricia (R) presenting their books at the Monsters and Miracles exhibit at the Skirball Cultural Center of Los Angeles, California, on May 16, 2010.